HAPPY, HAPPY CHINESE NEW YEAR!

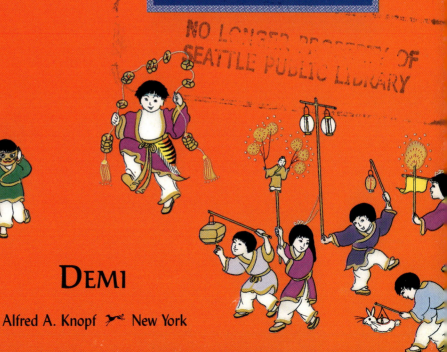

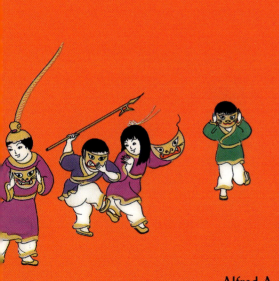

DEMI

Alfred A. Knopf  New York

plow

sow

plant

reap

pound

thresh

sift

store

IT'S SPRING!

The Chinese New Year falls during China's springtime.
(In the Western calendar, Chinese New Year usually takes
place in January or February.) For thousands of years,
China has been an agricultural country, and the people
are in harmony with the seasons and the cycles of planting
and harvesting. The Chinese New Year celebrates the
season for planting, as well as all new beginnings.

SWEEP AND DUST!

Part of getting ready for the Chinese New Year is making sure your home is neat and clean before the new year arrives. Tidy up your house and your room. Sweep out the old and bring in the New Year!

Now is also the time to get new seeds for planting.

mop

dust

scrub

brush

sweep

polish

wash

MAKE A FRESH START!

Wash your hair and get a new haircut. Buy some new clothes.
Pay the debts that you owe and collect what is owed to you!
Catch up on your homework!

COOK!

The New Year festivities include a feast on New Year's Eve. Everyone helps prepare the special foods that will be served. These foods have special meanings and are symbols of what is wished for in the year to come.

New Year's cakes and candies represent — peace and harmony, Chuen-ho.

— Candied melon, Jen, symbolizes wealth, virtue, growth, and good health.

Taffy candy, T'ang-kua, is for the Kitchen God, Tsun Kuan. —

— Mandarin cakes, Sa-ch'i-ma, represent all wishes fulfilled.

Puffed rice cakes, Mi-t'ung, stand for a sweet new year. —

— Pudding cake, Nien-kao, stands for a lucky new year.

Rice dumplings, Chiao-tzu, mean good fortune and heavenly blessing. —

— Fried rice symbolizes harmony and plenty, Chao-fan.

Steamed buns, Man-t'ou, stand for good luck and good fortune. —

— Fish symbolizes surplus, Yu.

Oysters represent good fortune, Hao-shih. —

— Clams signify profit and good omens, Hsien.

Shrimp represent wealth and abundance, Hsia. —

— A pair of carp symbolize fame and fortune, Ming-li Shuang Shou.

Sweet-and-sour fish signifies surplus, Ch'o-yu Yu-yu. —

— Pan-fried fish means that luck is coming, Shih-lai Lien-tao.

Beef stands for strengthening powers, Chiao-tzu. —

— Duck represents happiness, Yuan Yang.

Pork brings wealth, K'ou-jou. —

— Chinese cabbage represents wealth, Pai-ts'ai.

Lettuce signifies wealth and riches, Sheng-ts'ai. —

— Seaweed, Fa-ts'ai, means "Happy New Year!"

Persimmons mean that all wishes will be fulfilled, Tang-kuo. —

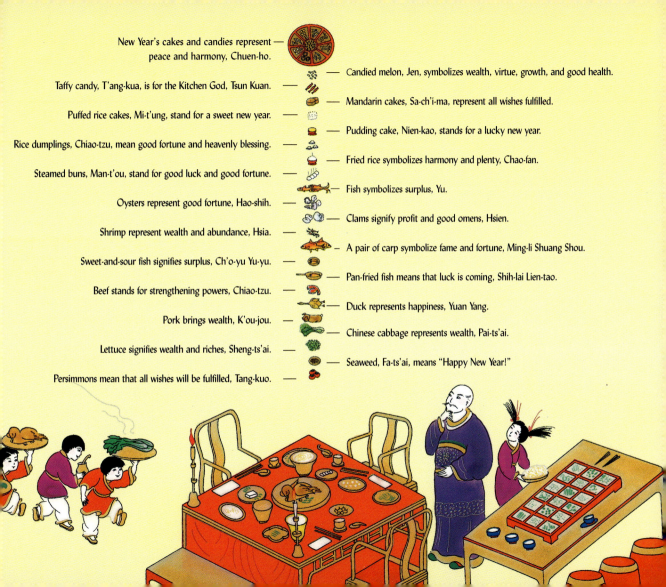

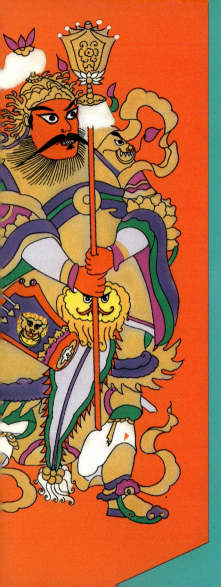

POP! POP! POP!

Firecrackers are an important part of the New Year celebration. The firecrackers are lit in front of each house, and the loud noises scare away the evil spirits. When the evil spirits have been scared away, the door guardians will make sure that the house is safe.

The door guardian
Yu-chih Kung,
protector from evil.

The door guardian
Ch'in Ch'iung,
protector from evil.

SWEET GIFTS!

New Year's Day is the time to visit family and friends. It is important to bring special gifts like melon seeds, flowers, candied fruit, and New Year's cakes to everyone you visit. Each gift brings with it special symbolic wishes for the coming year.

A tray of candies, called Chuen-ho, represents togetherness.
Candied melon will ensure growth and good health.
Candied lotus seeds will help to bring many sons into the family.
Candied coconut creates togetherness.
New Year rice cakes will sweeten your year.
And a gift of watermelon seeds is a wish for plenitude.

LION DANCES

For three to five days of the New Year, there are Lion Dances in front of stores to scare away evil spirits. The Lion Dances bring good luck!

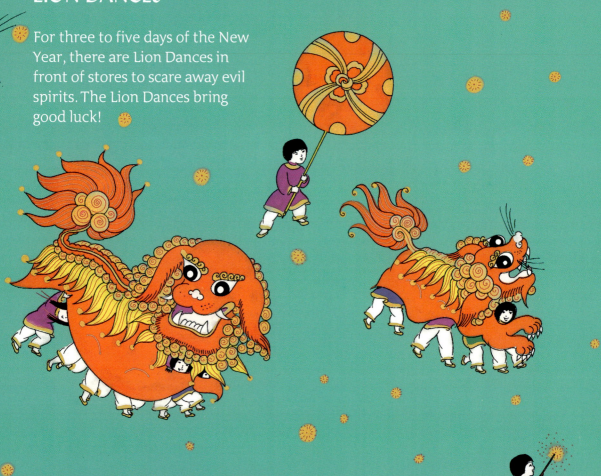

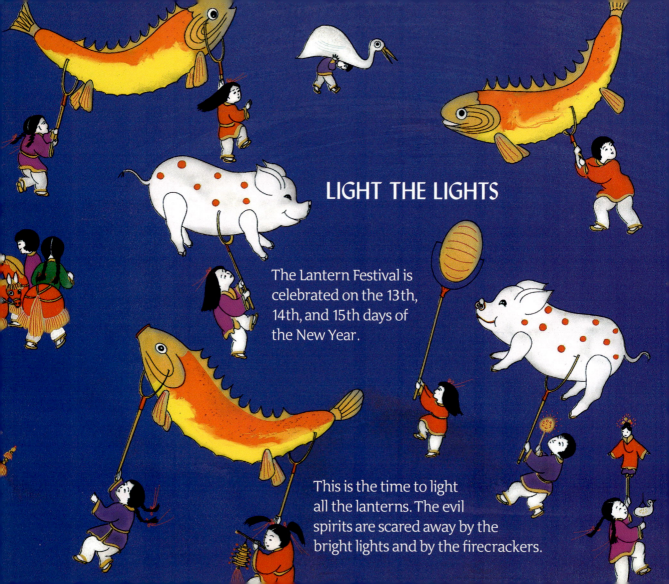

LIGHT THE LIGHTS

The Lantern Festival is celebrated on the 13th, 14th, and 15th days of the New Year.

This is the time to light all the lanterns. The evil spirits are scared away by the bright lights and by the firecrackers.

KUNG-HSI FA-TS'AI!
HAPPY NEW YEAR!

The Dragon Dances begin on New Year's Day and last for 15 days afterward, with drums and horns and happiness. Wishing you wealth, wisdom, and power and a wise Happy, Happy New Year!

THIS IS A BORZOI BOOK PUBLISHED BY ALFRED A. KNOPF

Copyright © 1997 by Demi
All rights reserved. No part of this book may be reproduced or transmitted
in any form or by any means, electronic or mechanical, including
photocopying, recording, or by any information storage and retrieval
system, without permission in writing from the publisher. • Published by
Alfred A. Knopf, an imprint of Random House Children's Books, a division of
Random House LLC, a Penguin Random House Company, New York.
Originally published in different form as *Happy New Year! Kung-Hsi
Fa-Ts'ai!* by Crown Publishers in 1997. Knopf, Borzoi Books, and the
colophon are registered trademarks of Random House LLC.
www.randomhousekids.com • *Library of Congress Cataloging-in-Publication
Data* • Demi. • Happy, happy Chinese New Year! / Demi. • p. cm. • Summary:
Examines the customs, traditions, food, and lore associated with the cele-
bration of Chinese New Year. • ISBN 978-0-375-82642-9 (trade) • 1. Chinese
New Year—Juvenile literature. 2. China—Social life and customs—Juvenile
literature. [1. Chinese New Year. 2. China—Social life and customs.] I. Title.
GT4905.D44 2003 • 394.261—dc20 • 2003043469 • Printed in Malaysia
November 2003 • 10 9 8 7